BAD APPLE

A Tale of Friendship

written and illustrated by

Edward Hemingway

PUFFIN BOOKS • **An Imprint of Penguin Group (USA)**

For best friends everywhere

PUFFIN BOOKS
Published by the Penguin Group
Penguin Group (USA) LLC
375 Hudson Street
New York, New York 10014

USA * Canada * UK * Ireland * Australia
New Zealand * India * South Africa * China

penguin.com
A Penguin Random House Company

First published in the United States of America by G. P. Putnam's Sons,
a division of Penguin Young Readers Group, 2012
Published by Puffin Books, an imprint of Penguin Young Readers Group, 2015

Design by Ryan Thomann.
Text set in Metallophile, Le Chat Noir, Pierre Bonnard, and a bit of Carrotflower.
The art was done in oils on canvas.

THE LIBRARY OF CONGRESS HAS CATALOGED THE G. P. PUTNAM'S SONS EDITION AS FOLLOWS:
Hemingway, Edward.
Bad apple : a tale of friendship / Edward Hemingway.
p. cm.
Summary: Relates how Mac, the apple, and Will, the worm, become friends.
ISBN 978-0-399-25191-7 (hc)
[1. Apples—Fiction. 2. Worms—Fiction. 3. Friendship—Fiction.] I. Title.
PZ7.H377436Ba 2011 [E]—dc22 2009046706

Puffin Books ISBN 978-0-14-751748-7

Manufactured in China

1 3 5 7 9 10 8 6 4 2

Mac was a good apple.

He shared his toys with the other apples,

helped Granny Smith pick up after art class,

and loved to dive fearlessly into the watering hole.

On a sunny day, Mac could bob for hours.

On cloudy days, Mac would search for the perfect pillow of green grass and take a long nap.

In his dreams it was always sunny. But one day, as Mac lay sleeping, it began to rain.

Soon all the little creatures in the earth around him poked their heads out to look for higher ground. Some of them found safety under the large toadstools.

Others crawled onto stones and pebbles. But one small worm had another idea.

When Mac woke up, he was covered in raindrops, and he wasn't alone.

You won't believe the dream I just had. A funny little worm was tickling me right here . . .

Will showed Mac
how to fly a kite,

fly himself,

and play in the dirt.

(He loved making a mess.)

Mac took his new
friend to the watering
hole to clean off.

He couldn't remember a better day.

Until he took Will to the orchard.

MAC'S A ROTTEN APPLE!

I'm not rotten. I'm . . .

. . . quite sweet, actually.

So they left.

Will cheered Mac up by reading aloud from some of his favorite novels.

(He was a bit of a bookworm.)

Mac liked the adventure stories best.

He also liked it when Will finished his sentences for him.

The most exciting part is when the pirates . . .

. . . find treasure in the dirt!

But the next day, it happened again.

And no one in the orchard would play with them. NOT EVEN the crab apples.

That night, the two friends sat alone on the grass without saying a word.

In the morning,
Will was nowhere
to be found.

Mac went back
to playing with his
orchard friends,

diving fearlessly into
the watering hole,

and painting in
Granny Smith's class.

But nothing was the same.

There was a hole in Mac that he couldn't fill.

Not a big hole. Just
a teeny, tiny little . . .

You know. A small hole
just big enough to fit . . .

(And nobody finished his sentences.)

In the dirt,

around the watering hole,

and—just when he had given up all hope—

he looked up in the sky.

Mac knew he'd rather be a Bad Apple with Will
than a sad apple without him.

Good and happy.

(And there's nothing bad about that.)